LoVe MonsteR

Rachel Bright

WELCOME TO
CUTESVILLE
Home of the fluffy

SCHOLASTIC INC.

This
is a monster.

(Hello, Monster.)

I think you'll agree,
he's a little bit funny-looking.

To say the least.

which makes being

funny-looking...

pretty,

darn

hard.

You might have noticed
that **everybody** loves

kittens...

and puppies...

and bunnies.

You know,
cute, fluffy
things.

But nObody lOves
a slightly hairy,
I-suppose-a-bit-gOogly-eyed
mOnster.

(POor MOnster.)

This might be enOugh to make a mOnster
feel, well, a bit doWn in the dumps.
But not being the mOping-aroUnd sort,

he decided to
set out and look
for someone who'd
love him,
just the way he was.

He looked high.

He looked low.

tumbleweed

He looked middle-ish.

He looked inside.

And outside.

More than once he thought that maybe ...

just maybe ...

he'd found what he was looking for.

But, as it turned out, things were
never quite as they seemed.

Yes, it would be
fair to say
that his search
did **not** go well.

And then it didn't
go well some more.

It didn't go well for such a long time, in fact,

that it began to get

dark.

And
Scary.

And, well,

not Very nice.

So the **monster**,
having lost **all** his Oomph,
decided it was time to give up.

BUS TO CUTESVILLE

and go hOme.

But in the blink of a gOogly eye . . .

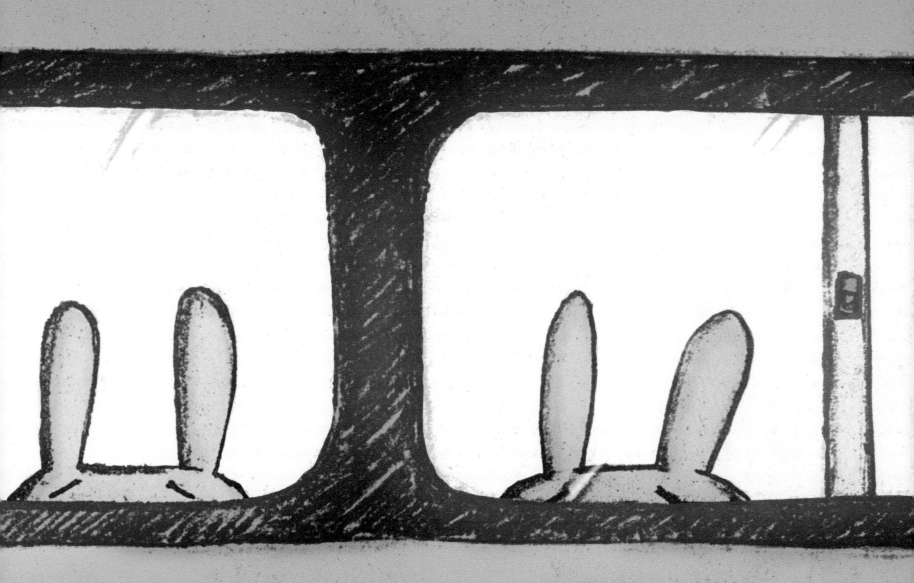

everything
Changed.

You see,
Sometimes,
when you least expect it...

love
finds you.

For the monsters who've found me
(& one slightly hairy one in particular)
—R.B.

WELCOME TO
CUTESVILLE
Home of the fluffy

and slightly hairy

PAINT

NAILS

And with Special
Wow-you're-amazing thank-yous to Mandy,
Nancy, Helen, Ann-Janine, Kayt, James & Rose

First published in Great Britain by HarperCollins Publishers Ltd.

ISBN 978-0-545-84810-7

12 11 10 9 8 7 6 5 4 3 2   15 16 17 18 19 20/0

Printed in the U.S.A.   08

This edition first printing, January 2015